HONEYBEE

Dipping into the flower zone
Honey stomach plump with nectar

Soaking up directions
Finding our ways in the dark

Fat little pollen baskets
Plumping our legs

You had no idea, did you?
You kept talking about

That wheelbarrow
And chicken

Round dance
Waggle dance

Only 5 species of honeybee
Among 20,000 different bee species

Out there in the far field
Something has changed but

You don't know what it is yet
And everything depends

On us

Naomi Shihab Nye

Honeybee

Poems & Short Prose

 Greenwillow Books

An Imprint of HarperCollinsPublishers

Gratitude to places where some of these pieces first appeared: *Bat City Review, Beloit Poetry Journal, The Café Review, Cutthroat, Court Green, Five Points, Great River Review, The Horn Book, The Midwest Quarterly, The Quirk, The San Antonio Express-News, Tikkun, Water-Stone Review,* and the Blue Star Nature Conservancy Project. "Parents of Murdered Palestinian Boy . . ." appeared on a broadside from Pyramid Atlantic Art Center. And thanks forever to Virginia Duncan, everyone at Greenwillow Books, Michael Nye, and Marie Brenner. Also Jim, Assef, Ignacio, Barbara, Rosemary, Karen, Roberto, and Hugh.

"Invisible" first appeared in a chapbook from The Trilobite Press.

"Last Day of School" first appeared in *After the Bell: Contemporary American Prose about School,* edited by Maggie Anderson & David Hassler.

❦ ❦ ❦

Honeybee

Copyright © 2008 by Naomi Shihab Nye

The text of this book is set in Nofret Light
Book design by Sylvie Le Floc'h

Library of Congress Cataloging-in-Publication Data

Nye, Naomi Shihab.
Honeybee : poems / by Naomi Shihab Nye.
    p. cm.
"Greenwillow Books."
ISBN: 978-0-06-085390-7 (trade bdg.) ISBN: 978-0-06-085391-4 (lib. bdg.)
I. Title. PS3564.Y44H66 2008 811'.54—dc22   2007036742

First Edition 10 9 8 7 6 5 4 3 2 1   Greenwillow Books

In memory of Aziz Shihab
1927-2007
our beloved father

and

Elizabeth Nye Sorrell
1909-2007
She loved poetry all of her days.
"In place of going to heaven at last,
I've been going there all along."

Contents

Honeybee   i

Introduction   1

✳

Your Buddy Is Typing   11

Someone You Will Not Meet   13

A Stone So Big You Could Live in It   16

Museum   17

For My Desk   22

Communication Skills   24

The United States Is Not the World   26

Taverne du Passage   27

Wee Path   28

Password   30

The Frogs Did Not Forget   32

Missing It   33

The Crickets Welcome Me to Japan   35

Ted Kooser Is My President   36

How We Talk About It   37

Culture of Life   39

Missing Thomas Jefferson   41

Don't Say   44

Running Egret   45

Lion Park   46

The Little Bun of Hours   48

Pollen   51

Honeybees Drinking   53

Weird Hurt   56

We Are the People   58

Help with Your Homework   62

Busy Bee Takes a Break   64

Bees Were Better   66

Invisible   68

Girls, Girls   70

What Happened to the Air   72

Slump   75

Deputies Raid Bexar Cockfight   77

Accuracy   79

This Is Not a Dog Urinal   81

Argument   82

There Was No Wind   84

Companions   85

For a Hermit   86

Letters My Prez Is Not Sending   89

Broken   92

The Cost   94

Friendly Postal Clerk, Saturday Morning   96

While You Were Out   97

Driving to Abilene in the Pouring Rain   98

Cinnamon Twist   99

Sunday   103

We Are Not Nothing   105

Our Best Selves   106

The Dirtiest 4-Letter Word   108

RSVP   109

Boathouse   110

The Problem of Muchness   112

How Do I Know When a Poem is Finished?   113

Excuse Me But   115

Bears   117

Pacify   118

To One Now Grown   120

Watch Your Language   121

Cat Plate   122

Click   124

Hibernate   125

My President Went   130

Texas Swing Low   132

From an Island   134

The White Cat   135

Ducks in Couples   137

Campaigning Door to Door   138

Parents of Murdered Palestinian Boy

    Donate His Organs to Israelis   140

Before I Read *The Kite Runner*   142

The First Time I Was Old   143

Useless   144

Jonathan's Kiwi Cake   145

Consolation   146

For Rudolf Staffel   147

Hot Stone Massage   149

Regular Days   150

Last Day of School   151

Young Drummer Leaving Alamo Music Company   158

The Room in Which We Are Every Age at Once   160

Gate A-4   162

Let the bees go honey-hunting
with yellow blur of wings
in the dome of my head,
in the rumbling, singing arch of my skull.

—Carl Sandburg
From "In Tall Grass"

Last night I dreamed—blessed illusion—
that I had a beehive here
in my heart
and that the golden bees were making
white combs and sweet honey
from my old failures.

—Antonio Machado
Translated by Robert Bly

Introduction

One of my favorite classes in college was a linguistics course called "The Nature of Language," in which students studied the language of animals. A few students not in the class made fun of us, mooing when they saw our notebooks. I selected bees as my focus for the semester, and our wonderful professor, Dr. Bates Hoffer, said this was a good choice, since bees are fabulous communicators. Bees can tell each other where the good flowers are—how far away, which direction to fly. They do jazzy dances. They can find their ways back to their own hives even if you try to block or trick them. Bees have memory and specific on-the-job task assignments and 900,000-neuron brains. I buzzed about the campus for a happy semester, researching in farm journals and encyclopedias, writing strange, dramatic papers, hoping to be stung.

What I do *not* recall studying was the growing industry of migratory beekeeping, in which beekeepers transport their hives long distances for pollination purposes. Maybe it wasn't happening much yet. The huge almond crop in California, for example, has in recent years been highly dependent on hired bees.

You now can read about industrious beekeepers who travel (it's not easy) the interstates with hundreds of hives in giant trucks. Good thing those bees can communicate. Maybe they're saying, "Where are we now? When's my time off?"

I also don't recall learning much about bee *problems*, though bees certainly had experienced struggles in their communities already and could be victimized by everything from funguses to viruses to mites.

During the spring of 2007, bee woes made continual headline news in the United States. Many reports said at least one third of the honeybees in the United States had mysteriously vanished. A grieving South Texas beekeeper was shown slumping sadly in his field of empty hives. Florida and Oklahoma recorded their sorrows. Anderson Cooper did a late-night special on CNN. Honey prices rose. There was lots of speculation about what was happening to bees, but no single answer or remedy.

I collected theories. Were pesticides, or nasty varroa mites, which had swept the bee nation, most responsible? Could it be changing weather conditions or cell phone beams? Obviously the current atmosphere sizzles with more electronic signals than any world of the past . . . I was ready to pitch my cell phone out. Something called "colony collapse disorder" was often cited as a possibility. Seemed like a parallel for human beings in times of war. War is no blossom.

The ongoing Bee Tragedy Stories remain inconclusive. I called Dr. Hoffer after decades and he agreed it's a troubling topic. Some people say "no big deal"—this fits into the cyclic pattern of nature—other insects or species of bees will pollinate where the honeybees leave off. But Dr. May Berenbaum, head of the department of entomology at the University of Illinois, says, "Though economists differ in calculating the exact dollar value of honeybee pollination, virtually all estimates (of losses to crops, etc.) range in the billions of dollars." That can't be good.

So, I've been obsessed. This is what happens in life. Something takes over your mind for a while and you see other things through a new filter, in a changed light. I call my friends "honeybee" now, which I don't recall doing before. If I see a lone bee hovering in a flower, I wish it well.

**

As for the "busy bee" thing, the word "busy" fell out of my vocabulary more than ten years ago. I haven't missed it at all. "Busy" is not a word that helps us. It just makes us feel worse as we are doing all we have to do.

Anyway, why are we rushing around so much? The common phrase "I can't wait" has always troubled me. Does it mean you want your life to pass more swiftly? This or that future moment will surely be better than the current moment, right? The moment we are living in may be lovely, but if we "can't wait" for some other time, do we miss it? We are honeybees in our own lives. But we forget.

Antonio Machado, the brilliant poet from Spain, dreamed a beehive in his heart could turn even flaws into something tasty. This interests me a lot. One thing becoming another, in the tradition of alchemy . . .

We are trained to work for success, but failures, mistakes, or disasters may lead us in intriguing new directions. As a young man, Rudolf Staffel forgot to sign up early for a painting course in Mexico and was stuck taking the pottery course. His whole life swerved. He became one of the great ceramic artists of the twentieth century.

Tim Duncan, the star of the San Antonio Spurs basketball team, was a swimmer when he was growing up. He practiced all the time. But a hurricane devastated the pool on his home island of St. Croix. It wasn't his *own* failure but the pool's demise which helped lead him to huge success in a different sport.

Are the honeybees cooking something up behind the scenes? How many writers or artists have said they stumbled into their favorite works when something else they were trying to create didn't succeed?

In Holyoke, Massachusetts, a vintage restaurant called Nick's Nest has been serving hot dogs, baked beans, potato salad, and popcorn since 1921. The slogan of the restaurant is "The Nest of Delicious." When my friend and I saw it one day, as we sped by in the rain on our way to eat in another town, I shouted, "Stop! I have to see that place! Look, it's totally old-fashioned!"

She said, "I thought we wanted Indian food."

We stared at the menu on the wall. My friend said, "See, they serve mostly hot dogs and you're a vegetarian. . . . I don't see any tofu pups on the menu." She was right. There was no entrée to suit me. We were in a vegetable curry mood. But my eyes drank in the countertop, the funny signs, the little booths with old jukeboxes still attached to the tables, and I knew, even though we didn't eat there, I would remember Nick's Nest forever. (Luckily another friend has now sent me a Nick's Nest T-shirt, so I can belong to it in spirit anyway.) *Drinking it in.* That's when we really live. Dipping and diving down into the nectar of scenes. Tasting, savoring, collecting sweetness . . . if you're in Holyoke, would you please go eat there for me?

My niece in Australia told me that the students in her university class were required to read the blog of an Iraqi citizen and write about it before they could graduate. She chose a girl who is now fifteen writing under the pseudonym Sunshine. I began reading Sunshine's blog too. I love the way she writes about details of her life—her friends, the books she is reading, her activities and memories. Life is so difficult since the war started, but still she ends her entries with lines like, "Try not to lose hope." She wishes she could live the way kids in other countries live, without so much constant violence surrounding them.

Sunshine has become my personal hero, drinking deeply out of the moments she is given, even when she wishes they were different moments. So much is passing so fast. . . .

My husband's cousin's husband, a man named Dee, who lives in Houston, recently sent out an e-mail survey asking people where and when was the last time they had seen a lightning bug. He remembered sitting on his Texas front porch as a boy, seeing hundreds of lightning bugs blinking around him. I had wondered about the lost lightning bugs over the years myself, and blamed their disappearance on pesticides. Many young people in the United States have never seen one and don't know what they do. (Why aren't the mosquitoes disappearing, by the way? Are they so much heartier than lightning bugs and honeybees?)

Dee's correspondents in far-flung little towns like Rosebud and Rockdale, Texas, replied that they were lucky still to have lightning bugs, but people in cities were all missing them. They remembered droves and crowds of them, the great American sport of capturing lightning bugs in jars with holes punctured in the lids and letting them go again. I wrote that the first time our son saw a lightning bug, when he was about six, in the Texas hill country, he insisted it was carrying a small kerosene lantern.

Here's a hope that we don't lose any more of the small things that blink in our darkness. Albert Einstein allegedly said, "If all the honeybees disappear, human beings have four years left on earth." We'd better increase our levels of attention.

Facts about insects and animals feel refreshing these days, when human beings are deeply in need of simple words like "kindness" and "communicate" and "bridge." Turtle organs do not deteriorate as a turtle ages. A shrimp's heart is in its head. Our cat just said, "Outside" and meant it, as a squirrel, swinging upside down from the bird feeder beyond the window, announced he is really a bird in disguise.

Your Buddy Is Typing

Your buddy in the early hours. Your buddy with the scratchy throat who didn't sleep well. On the other side of the earth he is rising, making a single cup of coffee, sitting down at a small wooden table. Your buddy who hasn't shaved in weeks. Your buddy in Nuevo Laredo missing the old days the easy crossings of borders the wanderings in streets without fear. Your buddy who doesn't want to see any bullets is typing a letter he will not sign. Your buddy with the aching wrist. Your buddy with high hopes watching sun come up over calm water thinking, we'll make it, maybe. Your buddy who sends 17 letters in 14 days. A surge of random observations but nothing is random. No one alone. The bold buddy and the shy one with a closet of stacked pages. The young buddy whose grandfather the great writer has been hiding for years. Your buddy in Japan who wishes your heart to feel like a primrose. Your buddy in Glasgow eating a radish as he types in golden light. Your buddy in a head scarf begging for sense. Your buddy in a sari who bosses the men. Your buddy who types with three fingers like you do. Your buddy in Australia your weary buddy in the airport lounge your buddy in the village library your buddy in the wireless hotel room where even the rod under the clothes lights up your buddy on the brink your buddy who was reminded what words could do after he swore they could do nothing anymore your buddy in Bethlehem who wonders if anyone listens your buddy who is feeling weak your buddy who tells what is really going on behind the scenes your buddy who refuses to back down your lost buddy who won't speak to you punishing you for reasons unknown even she must be typing to someone else by now, trust in this as you say good-bye give it up, typing will help you get through it no matter where you are when the restaurants close and the little shops you loved bolt their doors for the last time and the artist you wish you'd known better dies suddenly, you grip the memory of minor messages sent back and forth only months ago. Who else should you be typing to right now? Who else is on the way out? All of us. Everyone typing in the late and early in the far reaches in the remote unknowns in the heart of the diagnosis near the fishing huts with CATCH OF THE DAY signs the names of fish scrawled on blackboards by the whispering sea. ✹

Someone You Will Not Meet

Rolls her socks into balls,
lines them in a shoebox.

Sharpens a yellow pencil
carefully checking the point.

There used to be plenty of pencils.

Stares into a mirror thinking *fat nose, fat nose.*

Pins a green bow to her head,
plucks it off again.

Worries about loud noises.

Wraps presents in the same crumpled paper
over and over again for members
of her own family.

Gives her brother an orange because
he likes them more than she does.

He complains, *I am sick of this life.*
She fusses at him, *Don't say that.*

Gives her mother a handwritten booklet
made of folded papers called
One Apartment.

The people she loves most are in it.
The uncles who come and go are in it.
Lucky ducks.
They are afraid every time they go
but they brave it.

A few cats and plants and rugs are in it,
square television set with a scrappy picture,

and the streams of bees swooping
to the jasmine vine
right outside the window.

They dip into blossoms and fly away.
Never could she have imagined being jealous
of a bee.

She listens to the radio say there will be
more fighting
though no one she knows likes fighting.

Does anyone feel happy after fighting?

It's a mystery.

She chews on a sesame cookie
very very slowly.

Staring at the sesame seeds
she could almost give them
names. ✲

A Stone So Big You Could Live in It

It happens in the woods
A laugh just pops out
It happens with a stone so big you could live in it
Round mounds of soil and stone
Perfectly dressed in radiant moss
Blaze of bees around a single blooming branch
Path so quiet one foot answers the other
Charred ashes by Jericho Bay
Blue dots on trees lining the trail
Sudden sweetness of it
Someone was here before you
Didn't want you to get lost
Thank you
Someone
Thank you
Blue ✻

Museum

I was 17, my family had just moved to San Antonio. A local magazine featured an alluring article about a museum called the McNay, an old mansion once the home of an eccentric many-times-married watercolorist named Marian Koogler McNay. She had deeded it to the community to become a museum upon her death. I asked my friend Sally, who drove a cute little convertible and had moved to Texas a year before we did, if she wanted to go there. Sally said, "Sure." She was a good friend that way. We had made up a few words in our own language and could dissolve into laughter just by saying them. Our mothers thought we were a bit odd. On a sunny Saturday afternoon, we drove over to Broadway. Sally asked, "Do you have the address of this place?" "No," I said, "just drive very slowly and I'll recognize it, there was a picture in the magazine." I peered in both directions and pointed, saying, "There, there it is, pull in!" The parking lot under some palm trees was pretty empty. We entered, excited. The museum was free. Right away, the spirit of the arched doorways, carved window frames, and elegant artwork overtook us. Sally went left, I went right. A group of people seated in some chairs in the lobby stopped talking and stared at us.

✳✳

"May I help you?" a man said. "No," I said. "We're fine." I didn't like to talk to people in museums. Tours and docents got on my nerves. What if they talked a long time about a painting you weren't that interested in? I took a deep breath, moved on to another painting– fireworks over a patio in Mexico, maybe? There weren't very good tags in this museum. In fact, there weren't any. I stood back and gazed. Sally had gone upstairs. The people in the lobby had stopped chatting. They seemed very nosy, keeping their eyes on me with irritating curiosity. What was their problem? I turned down a hallway. Bougainvilleas and azaleas pressed up right against the windows. Maybe we should have brought a picnic. Where was the Moorish courtyard? I saw some nice sculptures in another room, and a small couch. This would be a great place for reading. Above the couch hung a radiant print by Paul Klee, my favorite artist, blues and pinks merging softly in his own wonderful way. I stepped closer. Suddenly I became aware of a man from the lobby standing behind me in the doorway.

"Where do you think you are?" he asked. I turned sharply. "The McNay Art Museum!" He smiled then, and shook his head. "Sorry to tell you. The McNay is three blocks over, on New Braunfels Street. Take a right when you go out of our driveway, then another right." "What is this place?" I asked, still confused. He said, "Well, we thought it was our home." My heart jolted. I raced past him to the bottom of the staircase and called out, "Sally! Come down immediately! Urgent!" I remember being tempted to shout something in our private language, but we didn't have a word for this. Sally came to the top of the stairs smiling happily and said, "You have to come up here, there's some really good stuff! And there are old beds too!" "No, Sally, no," I said, as if she were a dog, or a baby. "Get down here. Speed it up. This is an emergency." She stepped elegantly down the stairs as if in a museum trance, looking puzzled. I just couldn't tell her out loud in front of those people what we had done. I actually pushed her toward the front door, waving my hand at the family in the chairs, saying, "Sorry, ohmygod, please forgive us, you have a really nice place." Sally stared at me in the parking lot. When I told her, she covered her mouth and doubled over with laughter, shaking. We were still in their yard. I imagined them inside looking out the windows at us. She couldn't believe how long they let us look around without saying anything, either. "That was really friendly of them!" "Get in the car," I said sternly. "This is mortifying."

The real McNay was fabulous, splendid, but we felt a little nervous the whole time we were there. Van Gogh, Picasso, Tamayo. This time, there were tags. This time, we stayed together, in case anything else weird happened.

We never told anyone.

Thirty years later, a nice-looking woman approached me in a public place. "Excuse me," she said. "I need to ask a strange question. Did you ever, by any chance, enter a residence, long ago, thinking it was the McNay Museum?"

Thirty years later, my cheeks still burned. "Yes. But how do you know? I never told anyone."

**

"That was my home. I was a teenager sitting with my family talking in the living room. Before you came over, I never realized what a beautiful place I lived in. I never felt lucky before. You thought it was a museum. My feelings changed about my parents after that too. They had good taste. I have always wanted to thank you." **❀**

For My Desk

We judge books
by their covers
every day.

You do, I do.

Human beings—
we're stuck with ourselves.

Always working on
that new project.

Never keeping up or catching up
with what we miss.

Feeling remiss.

        Each morning
birds speak first.

Sparrows gossip joyously.

Gray dove continues to land on a feeder
too small for her.

A purple martin mother
and purple martin father
solve it all. ❀

Communication Skills

I am working on speaking to the ones
who haven't spoken to us in years,
the ones swinging punches out of nowhere,
the ones who decided to shun us
for reasons unknown,
who wouldn't greet our group
at the family reunion
but sat across the swimming pool
looking wounded.

The strength of strangers will
help us survive.
Strangers are so generous.
They don't know our faults, our flaws,
so they hope for the best,
muttering good morning
when you pass at the bridge.
The consolation of strangers
is endless and forgiving.

But it takes all our courage
with close ones sometimes.
Families, neighbors, best friends . . .
Even if we believe in world peace,
they will find reasons to dislike us.
I think of Gandhi who said
he might never have become
an activist for nonviolence
if the neighbor boys had not
beaten him up.   ❋

The United States Is Not the World

and this I was reminded of by
    mamas in silk saris
    grandpas in burgundy turbans,
      smoky overcoats
    Sikh boys with powder-puff topknots
    braided girls munching Belgian chocolate
    and a gloomy little lad with a strange
      golden cone on his head

    Thank you, I said. O thank you Gate
      D-4, Amsterdam to Delhi
    months of smug Americana dissolving
      quickly
    as tiny white no-jetlag pills
      on the tongue ✳

Taverne du Passage

Rush of rain,
ancient signature on earth.
In the old photographs, a boy with long hair
tips a basket of warm eggs toward the lens.

What do we retain?
There's a stained baby shirt
in my drawer. A music box
with a baby lifting its hands.

I miss so many things,
the deep indentations
in each hen's hay,
the way he said "precious"
and "gems," two words no longer living
in his coop. ❀

Wee Path

In the town of Robert Burns called Dumfries, one of the many towns in southern Scotland that claim the beloved bard who lived so large (many children, many loves), I took a wrong turn, walking. Missed the red sandstone landmark church, kept going by the River Nith, Robert's river he tramped along regularly, never imagining (I would think not) a white statue of himself in the center square. I walked till it was clear I was not getting anywhere I needed to be. Got a little nervous. Stopped to ask two Scottish men in checkered shorts who chorused conflictingly *go forward—nay, go back! I noticed you,* said one, *as I was driving home, and you looked lost.* One said, *go right,* the other *go left,* go up, go in, go out, till the younger said, *Okay listen to him.* Him said, *Take a wee path. You'll barely see it. There's a donkey in the field on the right. A donkey? Aye, a donkey. There are leaning trees, leaning like a cover for the path. Go between them. It's truly wee, I tell ye. Look hard. Walk between the walls and the fence and you'll find yourself right there, right there!* They wished me well. Younger said, *If you get lost, it's all his fault.* No donkey was spotted but dozens of rabbits cavorting on a wide flat green. And no single wee path but twenty perhaps and as for leaning trees, weren't there groves in all directions? Oh Robert Burns, I got lost in your land, a little lonesome, but I felt your poems in the soles of my feet. ❁

Password

I have made so many mistakes
you might think I would sit down

Here when it rains
the streets fill up like rivers
A woman swirls away in her Italian car
and the whole city mourns
They say she could sing
till something that might not have happened
had a chance again
You know, that gift we give
one another

How can we help someone else
want to live?
The man who sprays trees
stands beneath his hose
bathing in poison
He says a mask gets in his way

Here the roses stay on the branch
till sun steams their petals
like blackened collars

I miss the evenings
we walked among train tracks
reading messages in the weeds
even the strangest parts of ourselves
growing dear

A child awakens crying for candles
Those little tiny skinny ones he says
meaning incense sticks
He wants to clutch them in his bed

I have slept so many times
you might think I would really be awake
by now ❀

The Frogs Did Not Forget

how to do what they do
through the huge dry days
where were they hiding?
one might lose a tune   abandon a tradition
fall into a crack   but the frogs after the rain
were singing on six notes
outside the bedroom window's
tangle of vines
pleasure poking its throaty resonance
back into   my brain ✳

Missing It

When I was a teenager, my family drove hundreds of miles from Texas to the Grand Canyon, stopping at small Route 66 motels and diners, buying tea and lemonade in tall cups to keep us going. Seems to me we should have been reading Grand Canyon guidebooks in the car, but I think we were reading novels, newspapers, and magazines, and my mom kept doing crossword puzzles, constantly asking us for esoteric three-letter words. At a roadside stop, a wasp stung my brother in the neck. He said it was a bee, but I had seen it, A WASP. His neck swelled. Our parents worried. He had no experience of ecstasy, however, as I once had upon being stung in the neck vein by a WASP myself. By the time we arrived at our destination, I found myself wrapped around a squishy pillow in the backseat with a thunderous headache. My father woke me, told me to get out to look and see, and for a moment I couldn't remember where we were or why. Astonishing grogginess and crumpled clothes. I stumbled toward the edge of the Great View and noticed a man farther down the line with a raccoon on a leash. This woke me up. The raccoon seemed to be looking into the canyon, nose tipped forward. He turned his head side to side and sniffed, sat back on his haunches thoughtfully, and put his little paws together. I quietly eased in their direction. The man made some comment to the raccoon, like "Have we ever seen anything better, pal?" And the raccoon looked up at him and smiled. Perhaps I was hallucinating from my headache. I motioned to my family to join me at my eavesdropper's perch, but they had moved off toward a better angle between the trees. I could hear my mom's voice exclaiming, "It's so deep! Look how wide!" But I had so many questions I wanted to ask the man, like "How long have you been together, where did you get him, are you tempted to let him return to his own tribe, did he really just smile," etc. I could only stare into their reverie from a distance. It didn't seem right to break it. Later, driving home, as my family argued over whether they should have ridden down into the canyon on donkeys or not, whether we should have visited more vantage points or taken a guided hike, whether we should have stayed longer, found a motel room, *blah blah*. I realized I had not seen the layers of stone, the grandness of the Grand Canyon, at all. I had only seen the raccoon. ❊

The Crickets Welcome Me to Japan

All night they strum
their tuneless tunes

cousins of the crickets I heard
long ago in the corners of my room

I know the stories
to carry them out, not to crush them

and the small cages they are kept in
for good luck

but tonight I understand them
for the first time

after all my flying over water
the long tipped hours, the stretched-out light

they're saying, *Slow down*
slow down

We told you this long ago but
you forgot ✳

Ted Kooser Is My President

When I travel abroad, I will invoke
Ted's poems at checkpoints:
yes, barns, yes, memory, gentility,
the quiet little wind among stones.
If they ask, You are American?
I will say, Ted's kind of American.
No, I carry no scissors or matches.
Yes, horizons, dinner tables.
Yes, weather, the honesty of it.
Buttons, chickens. Feel free
to dump my purse. I'll wander
to the window, stare out for days.
Actually, I have never been
to Nebraska, except with Ted,
who hosted me dozens of times,
though we have never met.
His deep assurance comforts me.
He's not big on torture at all.
He could probably sneak into your country
when you weren't looking
and say something really good about it.
Have you noticed those purple blossoms
in a clump beside your wall? ❄

How We Talk About It

She's mourning her beloved lamb
found gutted and hanging from the rafters
of the high school barn.

How could anyone do such a thing?
Were they jealous of his prize?

He's mourning his son,
number 3000 American dead in Iraq,
but as far as he can feel, the worst one.

She says, "The lamb would have been killed later
after winning more animal shows, but nicely."

Now here is a place I pause
in wonder.

The father was grieved to see his son's picture
on an antiwar website.

Each morning the brain struggles to stay focused
on ones in front of it, ones with names,

but some rebellious streak
keeps sweeping the fields for those we won't hear
    about,

ragged & bloodied & hurriedly buried
pressed & jumbled & missed by someone else

we also won't know.
Look at this boy on the cover

of the magazine, with head in his hands.
What happened? He's called "a kid

whose village was destroyed," but
I don't think he's a kid anymore. ✽

Culture of Life

George W. Bush believes
in a "culture of life."

This is very interesting to those
who have recently died
because of his decisions.

They discuss it regularly.
What could they have done
    differently
 to be alive?

If only they had been born
 in another country
or lived in a different neighborhood,
the culture might have included them too.

Actually they liked life a lot.
They can't stop thinking about
their teacups and blankets.
The scent of sheep wool
in a warm room.

Click of almond shells
in a bowl.
That simple coming-home feeling
when someone happy to see you
greets you.
Never could they have imagined
being dead and thinking about teacups. ✿

Missing Thomas Jefferson

I am looking for a cry that feels big enough
A wind a mountain a grove of cypress trees
A human being saying something true
Not:
I will kill you today
So someone has a better life tomorrow

If we heard the cries so much like our own
The wailing I-am-burned sounds
I-am-nearly-dead-and-gone sounds
Who could keep blasting?

Help Me
Don't Hurt Me
This story has
No good parts in it

How many are desperate for a day of no explosions?
A sentence without someone's blood
At the end of it
Desperate for one wise person
To stand up bigger than rubble
And stop the rubble

What a lonely time we live in
Thomas Jefferson said *I not only write nothing on religion
but rarely permit myself to speak on it. . . . The genuine system
of Jesus and the artificial structures they have erected to make
them the instruments of wealth, power and preeminence
to themselves . . .*

I am looking for the human who admits his flaws
Who shocks the adversary
By being kinder not stronger
What would that be like?
We don't even know

Only the innocent shopkeeper led away in chains
The child drawing a dove
The mother bathing burned skin with a feathery cloth
Only they deserve the podium

A grace note and someone to sing it
"I'll be nicer to you than you are to me"
Everything we worked for
Every ethical tradition
Every bridge
More time to ease things out than to break them

Dipping into
Modern Eloquence
Volumes One Through Nine
Published 1900
I kept thinking how far
How far
We are
From there ❁

Don't Say

God said.
You made it up
then put it in God's pocket.
God may have thrown it out already. ❁

Running Egret

We want our nature to have a face.
An eye we can look into,
not like ours—clearer. Strong body
moving swiftly over land, belonging to no one.

Nonpartisan egret,
beyond everything that burdens us,
unexpected, unpredictable,
sheer motion—flash of white—
creatures with a silence
wider than our own.

There are days we wake and need an egret. ❊

Lion Park

Outside Johannesburg, the driver named Samuel and I drove slowly between vast meadows of zebras and small clumps of distant beige lions snoozing on their backs under trees. He said to me, "You want to do my favorite thing? We'll stop where there's no lion. And we'll stare out the window very patiently. All the cars behind us will stop, too. They will want to see what we see. And they will not be able to figure it out. We will point and their eyes will go where we point. If we wait long enough, something good may come into view. It is what I have found from my years of driving through this park. Stop where there is nothing to see and wait. Then you see something better. And trick people in the meantime."

"Fine!" I said. What a guy!

We stopped where there was nothing but a thirsty clump of grayish bushes and a puddle. And the car filled with Japanese travelers behind us stopped, too. And we pointed and peered. We did not open the windows as it is very important in lion parks not to open the windows. Everyone had mentioned the father who jumped out to take one quick picture the year before and was gobbled down in front of his kids. We pointed and the people behind us stared and stared. They looked curious and frustrated. A few clouds floated by. And then, under the wide South African sky, beside the scraggly bush, just as Samuel had predicted, a white lion stepped forth daintily from a shadowy hiding place, stepped right into the road beside us, ignoring us as if we were not there, and began drinking from the puddle in the road with a long lion tongue. We could see the ripples of muscle under her skin. We could count the toes on her feet. ❋

The Little Bun of Hours

Days that felt like sheet cakes in long silver pans
frosted or not, plenty of cake no matter
    who appeared,
a sift of powdered sugar, and the knife
laid casually by. Maybe a sack of French bread
broken in half. I liked the small stacked plates
on the counter, the way you drove around in a box
without going anywhere. We could send
the bears to school and write notes for them
to take home to their mothers, who were camels
and rabbits. Sometimes I looked at a clock.
When you were four, lightning cracked my brain
and I could see all the way till now, this fist of days
before you leave. It took away my sleep,
    my confidence,
who were we before you? Though of course
there had been more of those years. . . .

When Cyrus says, "Just don't breathe down his neck,
    okay?"
I am hanging onto the little bun of hours,
wrapping it in the softest napkin,

tucking it into every pocket,
though you don't see it, you are never hungry
now. The locusts thrumming their summer blues
    sound old.
If Jesus had died by an axe, would Christians carry axes around?
You always asked the best questions.
This conversation is not finished.
Remember how the stories had many endings,
you laughed when we changed them.

Take your laundry baskets, your first-aid kit,
but don't take my failings, okay? Forget the times
I snapped, or had no patience, okay?
And I will try to remember
when you liked me more than when you didn't.
It is the butter on the bread. ❊

Pollen

Sometimes in the mornings
a sense of knowing tickles my windows,

mechanical thud outside,
gears shifting, engine waking up

like a bee doing its waggle dance
in front of the hive.

Even if I don't know what that yellow machine
means, exactly, it companions me.

Man in a bucket, examining high light,
repairing wires nibbled by a squirrel.

The world's at work in the hopeful hour,
things put together

won't be blown apart,
dissolve or disappear.

Did you know bees ventilate their homes
by hovering outside and fanning their wings?

Light passes through thinking,
helps us find the field again. 🐝

Honeybees Drinking

When did your language spring alive? At two, single words chipped awake, precious gems in the cave of the holy mouth. *Pajama* could hypnotize. I lay on the grass beneath the clothesline's flapping pajama pants singing sweet three-buttoned glory, a nectar in the remembering and repeating, till lost in bliss. *Like a swoon in a flower, basking, collecting* . . . Someone nodded, responded, recognizing the fat little bee-body of syllable, *yes, yes, she said it, did you hear what she said?* Words and voices, hovering, dipping down . . . how few people we know in the beginning. Parents, grandparents, vegetable man, the woman called Caroline at the farm up the hill, pronounced like "line"—*a clothesline in her name.* Big blue-jean pants were strung on it, no flowery aprons. She sold strawberries in little pint boxes, shooed chickens, arranged zucchini by size. She said she didn't love the farm, though, didn't even love vegetables, she only loved the man who loved it. *Wrap a word in another word* . . . so she lived with him and worked the ruddy acres, in the steaming heat. Heat felt pointed in those days—it had a nose on it. Things would be made clearer as years went by—the level of irony one voice can contain. Sometimes, the voices around you were voices in your conscience. *Does it sound like anyone you know or is it only yourself?* Caroline's odd frank voice was one of mine. It never dressed up. It told things directly, beat-down hoe to a clump of earth. *Humph!* She bent over in muggy field laboring hard under sun till she couldn't stand up straight anymore, and of course her farmer husband died first and left her with the acres. Insult upon injury. Now what? By then you're devoted to the system, you can't just move. Tangle of blackberry vines, ruin of beautiful barns, battered crates, fourteen cats, ripe compost, and the white delivery truck with ORGANIC rusting off the side.

Fifty years later her fields are overgrown except the one in which a man from down the block is growing pumpkins and sometimes I fly over them. I look down past the ragged line of trees just beyond the airport and see them, rumpled, marked with the lines of old crops and weeds. And the tears roll out of my eyes streaking the inside of the airplane window. I still call her on Sundays sometimes to say, "What's up? Is anything up?" which is really strange if you've been doing it so long and especially if you're calling someone on a farm.

Usually she says, "Not a thing." Then tells me some disappeared cat or barking dog story. But one day she says, "You know what? Everything was *so* dry this year that the poor honeybees were drinking water out of the cats' water bowls under the chins of the cats. Can you imagine? I never even knew bees drank water, I thought they just drank flower juice. How desperate they must have been! Sneaking in under the big tongues and teeth of the cats like that?"

Weird Hurt

Because the person behind me on the plane kept kicking my seat, across the long striped blue/brown geological wonder of Colorado to California, I turned around to stare at her finally through the crack and somehow pulled a muscle in my leg. How someone can strain a leg muscle while not even standing up beats me. But it definitely follows the usual pattern of getting hurt when we are rushing, jostled, distracted, mindless, otherwise off the beam. I was distracted in the plane. Trying to read a book and bumping. (Last summer I broke my little toe while running to answer a telephone on the eve of leaving to Scotland—a hiking tour became a hobbling tour in one swift second. A hammer once fell on my head off the top of a ladder when I was planning a small person's birthday party. *Jostled, distracted . . .*)

Pay attention takes on new meanings out in the world.

Honeybees have been hauled all over agricultural creation by their owners in wooden hives to pollinate flowers far from the ones they grew up with. Even if they only grew up a little while ago. Honeybees live and dive and drink in the same fields where poisons are sprayed. To escape decline for any time at all would seem like a miracle. Incidentally, to call a time in history a "time of war" when there would not have been a war if you did not make one seems somehow disingenuous— it was hardly inevitable, as a severe thunderstorm might be. Bees are fine in severe thunderstorms, apparently. Could the bees with their profound radar beams and personal sensitivities be mirroring the disarray in the world of humans? Watch your step. Mind your head. A news story about movies for last season announced proudly, "HORROR/SLASHER FLICKS TO FILL YOUR SCREENS."

We Are the People

always going somewhere else. What is this peculiar attribute of our households, our days, our nation? We will not be here long enough to get tired of it. Does this make us less responsible? It's that relationship you have with a *towel* when the towel belongs to a *hotel.*

If we can't go anywhere else, are we more encouraged to enhance and protect the place where we are? Hmmmmm. Bzzzzzzz.

We should do all we can to stay out of jail, but now and then it is quite uplifting to pretend we are under house arrest.

I heard, if you spend less time at work (does this apply to school, too?) you do better work while there. Concentrated bursts enhance performance. Drop all the prefacing and wrap-up, and more gets done.

The frogs under the bridge in the Cairo park after dark had the best singing voices I have ever heard with frogs. They were not on tour. They sang that way every night, on the rim of the great city, its fabulously jumbled markets and shining domed mosques. The frogs were harmonizing, resonating so loudly you could feel a multi-layered frog chorus through your feet as well as your ears. Took a minute to realize it was frogs. It could have been buried bulldozers. With really well-oiled engines . . . I was still carrying my South African sugar packet with wisdom printed on it, "From contentment with little comes happiness."

In the old days, honeybees found their own pastures and meadows, clumps and clots of pollen. In the new days, their hives were carted by farmers here and there, intentionally. The bees were *rented out.* How this affected their stability and general constitutions may only now be emerging with the sudden total disappearance (no corpses) of a large number of honeybees in the world. I mean, if you get *rented out,* what does that do to your willpower? If you get *carted around,* what does that do to your radar?

I know people who, the minute they get into their homes, tell you where they are going next.

I am one of them.

This is nothing to be proud of.

I am trying something out. *Where are you going?*
Nowhere, nowhere at all.
It feels like an aberration.
But a certain calm descends upon the house.

One evening, after remembering there used to be a
lovely thing in the sky called a "sunset," I trundled to my
front porch, sat on the top step with an icy glass of
freshly squeezed limeade, some crushed mint leaves
thrown in for good luck, and waited. The western sky
rumpled and heaved, brewing elegantly, turning over,
graying and pinking all at once. Maybe it was too
cloudy for a sunset. Cars rolled past, going home from
work. What a comforting, sometimes lonely hour.

Streaks of red shot out from behind the gray rumples.
My neighbor walked past with her dog. "What's
wrong?" she called. I said, "What? Nothing." She said,
"Why are you sitting there like that?" I pointed at

the sky. She looked at it and shrugged. "Oh. You look locked out."

So ask yourself, you swirling tornado of a human being, in a world of disoriented honeybees,
do you want to look locked out the minute you sit down?
I ask you. 🐝

Help with Your Homework

Her e-mail message asked me please to write a two- or three-page essay on one of my poems. She would pick the poem. Then she said, "Please do your best work— this is half of my grade."

I kid you not. And she was a community college student, not a child.

We cannot begin to count our friends and helpers. Although I did not turn out to be her helper after all (hadn't I written the poems already and wasn't that *my* part of the homework?), I have no doubt she enlisted someone else. She had that air and *tone.* Some drones are so lazy they lie around in the beehive all day waiting for another bee to feed them. Passage of mind from thought to thought. Crevices of honeycomb stroked with sweetness. *Zip zip how long can we hover in any one zone?* The zen abbot suggested we try to *drop our inner commentary* as we took a hike up the hill to the memorial ashes site of Suzuki Roshi. Oh, but how deliciously and tenaciously the chatter stuck to the inner tiers of our brains. Later, meditating on a pillow, I absorbed the swishing of latecomers, the snuffling and sneezing of the sitter two pillows down, as hard as I tried to ignore them. (Why do people with colds always sit near me?) Buses on the street made heavy braking sounds at corners, but back in the mind's hive, chips and glimmers of language and emptiness sashayed gracefully side to side. ❦

Busy Bee Takes a Break

All the theories about the disappearing bees omit one possibility: they are sick of the word "busy." They are on strike. Sure this cycling and collecting and producing is what they've done for so long . . . worker and queen and drone . . . blossom and hive and comb . . . but the last thing the bees want stuck in their pollen baskets is a cliché. Busy? Not I. We can't even know if they adore the fragrances of flowers . . . but they must, right? Let's hope so. Let's hope there's pleasure in it.

In France, some teenagers asked me, "Is it true, in your country, students don't take time to sit down and drink tea and eat pie upon return from school?"

Eat pie? This was hard to answer.

"I hope they eat pie," I said. "We all need pie."
Then I started looking for a restaurant that served pie.

Down the street from my Texas home is one of those discount bread stores that sells 8–10 packaged pies for a dollar. *Cherry, coconut, apple, pecan.* They scare me. Pie should not be that cheap.

In England, the glossy catalogue tucked free inside the Sunday *Guardian* advertised, on one spread, products to help with the following problems: anti-frost mat, anti-mould mat, ultrasonic cat repeller, bark control collar, and mole chaser. I have to admit, none of these are things I have worried much about in my life, except maybe mould, spelled mold in the USA. But I have not worried about it inside my refrigerator, which is where the anti-mould mat is meant to be placed.

There are people we have never seen who are busy thinking up things we should be worried about.

How may we all be restored? Poor busy bee, wind down, wind down. "On average, one out of every four mouthfuls we eat or drink comes from plants that benefit from the services of a pollinator," says biologist Matthew Shepherd.

Watch us humans as we enter our rooms, remove our shoes and watches, and stretch out on the bed with a single good book. It's the honey of the mind time. Light shines through our little jars. 🦋

Bees Were Better

In college people were always breaking up.
We broke up in parking lots,
beside fountains.
Two people broke up
across the table from me
at the library.
I could not sit at that table again
though I didn't know them.
I studied bees, who were able
to convey messages through dancing
and could find their ways
home to their hives
even if someone put up a blockade of sheets
and boards and wire.
Bees had radar in their wings and brains
that humans could barely understand.

I wrote a paper proclaiming
their brilliance and superiority
and revised it at a small café
featuring wooden hive-shaped honey dippers
in silver honeypots
on every table.

Invisible

I used to walk out past the candle factory
where the whole air smelled like sweet wax
and the wall advertising BEE SUPPLIES
made me feel better, knowing that was
one more thing I would probably never need.
Far, far, till whatever was weighing me
shrank and the roses grew audible
in gardens again, nodding their heads.

At the library, hoboes read magazines,
they never sat together.
Tables spread with stock pages, metro news,
while the fat clock reeled off hours
and the hoboes returned to wherever they slept.
Once a hobo stood in my zinnias with his big feet,
said he was looking for the hose.
I said, "It's right behind you"
and he closed his eyes while drinking.

Sometimes, walking in the city,
I felt suddenly thirsty,
each storefront sparkling,
women at stoplights,

the glossy shine of their lips.
I wanted to enter restaurants with them
where the clink of words made business sound real.
Each time they swallowed, a waiter tensed,
moved towards them with the pitcher.
I wanted the small room between sentences,
the dark and wonderful room.
When they rose, waiter with towel
folded on arm standing expectantly by.
I wanted to feel that moment when
everyone disappears to one another,
she steps out swinging her pocketbook,
his hands return to his trousers
and the new tablecloth appears,
shaken free of its folds.

I could walk home again,
having seen that. The clouds would be
opening doors and windows above us.
I could cross a street and
step right through.

Girls, Girls

When the boys are alone,
they wash the dishes with facecloths.

When a honeybee is alone—rare, very rare—
it tastes the sweetness
it lives inside all the time.

What pollen are we gathering, anyway?
Bees take naps, too.
Maybe honeybees taste pollen side by side
pretending they're alone.
Maybe the concept "alone" means nothing
in a hive.

A bumblebee is not a honeybee.
It only pretends to be.

The cell phone in your pocket
buzzes against your leg.
It's not a honeybee though. It's just a
mining bee, or leaf-cutter, or
carpenter.

You're stung by messages from people far away.
You can't make anyone well.
You can't stop a war.
What good are you?

Bees drink from thousands of flowers,
spitting up nectar
so you may have honey
in your tea.

Maybe you don't want to think about it
so much.
Pass the honey please.

During winter, bees lock legs
and beat wings fast to stay warm.
Fifty thousand bees can live in
a single hive.
Clover honey is most popular
and clover is a weed.
All the worker bees are female.
Why is that no surprise?

What Happened to the Air

Well there were so many currents in it after a time,
so many streams of voices crisscrossing above
    the high pasture
when she went out to feed the horses, gusts of ringing
and buzzing against her skin. Sometimes near
    the biggest live oak
she paused to feel a businessman in Waxahachie
    calling out
toward his office in El Paso, a mother boarding
    a plane in Amarillo
waking up her Comfort girl. Hard to move sometimes
    inside
so many longings, urgencies of time and distance,
hard to pretend everything you needed was right
    in front of you,
bucket and feed and fence, that bundle of hay Otto
    pitched inside your gate,
that rusting tractor Juan might fix someday. You
    wished everything
were still right *here*, the way it used to be,
before honeybees were in jeopardy,

when the Saturday mystery episode streaming toward
    your radio
was the only beam you might ride from west to east,
before we were all so strangely connected
    and disconnected
inside a vibrant web of signals, and a crowded wind. 🐝

Slump

At a Halloween party, a person dressed as a baked potato says he is a filmmaker but has recently realized he is not very interested in films. He speaks in a confiding tone—sadly and softly—though I don't believe we have met before. It would be hard to know. His voice doesn't sound familiar. All I can see of him, besides dark eyes, is his aluminum foil wrapper. "It's really *intense* to discover your own work doesn't matter to you anymore," he mourns. He can't sit down, so he leans over me, where I am seated on the floor of the kitchen of someone's house, wearing a bathrobe. "What are you?" everyone asked when I entered, and I said, "Tired." The potato says he thought about coming as a honeybee but couldn't make the wings. This is the first year he really "bonded" with Halloween and he's surprised to have had any enthusiasm for it, since he feels so discouraged about everything else. "Maybe you just need to take a break," I say. "How did you decide to be a baked potato, anyway? It's very innovative." Everyone else has been asking him how many rolls of foil it took. Instead of answering, he asks how it is to be a poet. Goldilocks—or is it Dorothy?—walks into the kitchen and opens the refrigerator, revealing an incredible heaped-up stash of food—fruit bowls, cold shrimp, cheeses and dips—where only a white door was visible before. "About like that," I say. ❄

Deputies Raid Bexar Cockfight

Near the Atascosa County Line.
An anonymous tip. *Hello sirs, I just saw one hundred cars*
Pull up to the chicken pen.
Seizure of 368 roosters and hens called a state record.
Deputies also spotted about 200 spectators.
Many scattered into the woods,
some clutching roosters in their arms.
This is my favorite line in the story.
It is hard to run carrying a mean rooster.
One mean rooster is a huge dad-gum rooster.

Why is it such a relief to read this front page story?
How many of us could gather 200 friends
for anything? Would 200 friends show
for a great violinist?

There is no pretense in this story.
Now, the neighboring story about
the invasion of Iraq, that's different.
I attended one cockfight in my life,
a pitiful bloody display, so I wandered away
toward the Sierra Nevada mountains
till everyone else was ready to leave.

On that strange day
I pledged myself further to the strange life
I have been living ever since,
away from the ring, betting on nothing,
a friend of chickens in general, friend of dust
and lost hours in which everything distant
and near falls into clearer light. I won't say
it's wrong or right but it changed everything
for me. ✽

Accuracy

Lyda Rose walked through our front door and said, "Where is the sock monkey? I need him." This surprised me. She had never shown any interest in the sock monkey before.

We began digging in the tall basket where stuffed animals live.

Lyda Rose said, "I am two and a half now, did you know that? Where is he?"

We threw out the snake, the yellow bunnies, battered bears, a small eagle wearing a blue T-shirt, a camel, and the bird that makes a chickadee sound if you press its belly.

Sock Monkey was buried at the bottom.

Lyda Rose clutched him to her chest. "My husband!" she said, closing her eyes dreamily.

I was astonished. "Your husband? When did this happen?"

She spoke clearly and definitely. "I thought of him and I married him in my mind."

She ran around the dining room clutching her husband tightly, singing the song of a chickadee trapped in a human body.

"How great! I am so happy for you both!" I said, following her.

She did not answer, lost in a newlywed's swoon.

I said, "It is so nice that you love him now!"

And she stopped dancing, staring at me disapprovingly. "I didn't say I love him! I said, *he is my husband!*" ✽

This Is Not a Dog Urinal
(cardboard sign propped in leafy groundcover)

No. This is not a poop-pot, a cardiovascular rescue
device, a farmer's market.
This is not a beehive, a creek bed,
a parking lot, a back alley.
This is a frilly bush in someone's personal front yard
and that someone is *sick of it.*

Take your doggie elsewhere please.

Or we will be after you with garden shears
and shovels. Have respect for someone else's
lovely landscape dream which includes neither
a tribe of slippery snails,
your doggie,
or you. ❊

Argument

People were biting air,
snapping with smart opinions.
Everyone wanted to feel safe,
but no one would say that.
So they tried to act right instead.

For a thatched cottage
at the botanical gardens,
safety meant having a roof
water would run off,
in case of a storm.
A man traveled all the way
from England to thatch the roof.
It's a dying art.
He worked by himself
for three whole months.

Tiny windows,
cobblestone walk,
the roof smells of clean broom straw,
fresh air, meadowlands.

Now, when we stand inside it,
everything complicated
falls away. You think whatever you like,
okay? We don't have to match.
Look how the lattice of light
falls across all our feet. ✿

There Was No Wind

I don't know why I would tell
an outright lie
to someone I never saw before
but when she asked
Did you close this door?
in an accusing tone
I said *No, the wind closed it*

She gave me an odd look
pushed the door wide open
and left it that way

I felt strange the rest of the day
walking around
with a stone on my tongue ❋

Companions

She lived with words in a tall white house.
Hundreds of books lined her shelves.
They smelled like time, they smelled like rain.
Fanning the pages, she smiled.
I was ten when I found this friend.
Cherry pie steaming on top of the stove . . .
We sat till it was cool.

She lit up like a lantern when I rang.
Tell about your teachers, your work.
Who's the bad boy again?
Have you seen that dog that bit you under the eye?
The plates were stacked beside the pie.
Her husband had died before we were born,
but she didn't live alone.
She lived with words. ❀

For a Hermit

1.

The hermit Justiniani walked across Europe
after refusing to take his final vows.
He walked across the colonial United States,
coming to live in a cave in southern New Mexico.
Once he walked from Las Cruces
to San Antonio
for a little visit.

Justiniani led mystical prayer gatherings,
conducted healings in living rooms,
then walked 20 miles home
to his dwelling in the cave.
People worried he might not be safe,
living alone in those wild times,
as opposed to these,
sleeping without a lock,
or even a door.

He promised to light a fire every Friday night.
They could see it from town.
When the fire didn't appear,
he was found with a knife through his back,

wearing a thorny girdle of the *penitentes*,
"another unsolved murder" of those days.

Justiniani, pray for us,
our secret sorrows,
our inability to walk so far.
Pray for the signal fires we fail to light,
that we will have the power to light them.
Pray for the battered, unchosen people.
We have not come far at all
from your time.

2.

Your diary sleeps in untranslated Italian
in a locked glass case.

When I found out about it
I went a little crazy.

I need to know
what you knew.

3.

The ceiling of your cave is charred.
Along the path, clumps of cactus, desert flowers,
    chips of flint.
I stood inside, trying to imagine which way
    you slept in there,
pointed out or in, listening to the echo of birds
over Dripping Springs Road.
Please grant us the depth of your silence.
We are lost inside the world. ✻

Letters My Prez Is Not Sending

Dear Rafik, Sorry about that soccer game
you won't be attending since you now
have no . . .

Dear Fawziya, You know, I have a mom too
so I can imagine what you . . .

Dear Shadiya, Think about your father
versus democracy, I'll bet you'd pick . . .

No, no, Sami, that's not true
what you said at the rally,
that our country hates you,
we really support your move
toward freedom,
that's why you no longer have
a house or a family or a village . . .

Dear Hassan, If only you could see
the bigger picture . . .

Dear Mary, I'm surprised you have
what we would call a Christian name
since you yourself . . .

Dear Ribhia, Sorry about that heart attack,
I know it must have been rough to live
your entire life under occupation,
we're sending a few more bombs over now
to fortify your oppressors,
but someday we hope for peace in the region,
sorry you won't be there to see it . . .

Dear Suheir, Surely a voice is made to be raised,
don't you see we are speaking
for your own interests . . .

Dear Sharif, Violence is wrong
unless we are using it,
why doesn't that make sense . . .

Dear Nadia, I did not know about
your special drawer, you know I like
to keep a few things too that have meaning to me . . .

Dear Ramzi, You really need to stop crying now
and go on about your business . . .

Dear Daddo, I know 5 kids
must feel like a lot to lose in one swoop
but we can't stop our efforts . . .

Dear Fatima, Of course I have feelings
for your own people, my college roommate
was from Lebanon . . .

Dear Mahmoud, I wish I had time
to answer your letter but you must understand
the mail has really been stacking up . . . ✻

Broken

I broke my favorite glass today,
Habana Cuba it said in blue,
with a strange little etching of a ruin,
perfect for summer mint and lime.
Knocked its block off, right in the sink.
But it's a time of sorrow anyway,
one glass is nothing.
So many glasses
are smashed in the dirt.
Coffee cups, crushed to rubble.
Proud bridges, buildings, bookshelves,
we sign all the petitions
but bombs continue to blow.

A president who doesn't do everything he can
    to stop war
should break his own plates and see how it feels.
Should walk and cower and weep.
Should be wearing someone's borrowed clothes
and kissing his brother's broken face
by a pool where the dead are bathed.
A president who prefers wars to talking

should be bowing down in a schoolroom
where words on a wrecked wall whisper one last time,
Say it. Say it with language—noun, verb, adverb—
the ways words come together to make a line
someone might understand.

O Havana, I'm hoping to visit you soon,
hoping for your better days.
I want to see your buildings
before someone smashes them.
O Lebanon, I never got there yet,
and now we will never get
to what you used to be.
And to ancient Iraq, multitudes of people
and blocks we will never see—
no apology big enough.

It is hard to drink lemonade
without weeping into the glass,
the generic glass that reminds me of
nowhere we dreamed of going. ✻

The Cost

How deeply agreeable,
the word *read* appearing in
the word *thread*.

A church marquee in Wisconsin
asked, WHAT DOES IT TAKE
TO MAKE PEACE?

A lot, apparently.
We could start with all the elementary
school librarians and counselors

fired here last night
for "lack of funds."
Peacemakers, every one of them,

I'd place my money on it.
So many lives threading out into
the wilderness of adulthood

fortified by books and good advice.
Oh students, we will teach you
everything you need to know

then place a gun in your hands?
Makes sense, doesn't it?
No sense seems common anymore. ✽

Friendly Postal Clerk,
Saturday Morning

So what do poets do on
weekends

                huh?

I guess nuthin' much

                right?

I guess every day

is a weekend

to you? ✳

While You Were Out

A crow
with a yellow Post-it note

stuck to its beak
paused on the feeder
beyond the window
looked around twice
nodded its head
then flew away.

Big Day
at the office. ❊

Driving to Abilene in the Pouring Rain

From San Antonio to Abilene I never turned my windshield wipers off. That's four straight hours. The hills were flush with rain. Junction reminded me of a cinnamon roll three months ago. I turned my Bob Dylan CD up loud so I could hear it over the thunder. Bob kept me steady on the flooded two-lane. I passed Menard with its historic ditch. Big day for a ditch. In Eden I bought a juice called Nirvana and took a wrong turn. The girl said, *We have only one stoplight. . . .* but I missed it. Bob was not quite there yet but he was getting closer and closer. It was raining too hard to see. Then a massive silver cross in a field at Ballinger scared me, the way oversized things did when I was a kid. Why do people do that? Make things too big? This did not seem like the route I used to take. I pulled off to read the map. Where was Coleman? Where was that old windmill with only two blades? I used to sit around with kids in the Buffalo Gap cemetery and let them make grave rubbings. Now there were ugly subdivisions, big mistakes slapped up outside towns. Then I passed a restaurant where we once had the worst meal in the state of Texas and felt right at home again. ❋

Cinnamon Twist

We did not mean to hurt my mother's feelings when we filled out the application form in her name in response to the Help Wanted sign in the window of the bakery. She was startled to be called for an interview regarding a job to which she had not applied. We were trying to ease her loneliness. She & my father had recently moved to a different city, leaving both their children behind. She had not yet found many new friends or activities. My father & I were taking a walk together in the unfamiliar neighborhood, discussing her melancholia, when we saw the sign. It was not the first mistake in anyone's life. She could walk to work. Passing the groomed suburban houses in their impeccable isolation & the ragtag apartments & the cleaners & the video store & the grocery where the carts bunched up around the poles in the parking lot by early afternoon . . . wearing a hat against the serious Texas sun, perhaps a straw hat she might wear to work in a garden . . . carrying a purse with a wallet, a coupon for Handi-Wrap & one for cat food . . . what did you do in a bakery besides measure, mix, bake, arrange, slide new trays onto shelves, dust crumbs, talk to ladies wearing nice linen jackets or tank tops, take orders, fill sacks, make change? It sounded comforting. Sugar shakers and honey bears. Cake doughnuts or French? Glazed or powdered? We did not know about the secret album under the cash register that people would ask for in a glinting manner, or that our own mother would be asked to lift it forth & open it before their eyes, cakes shaped like breasts, single or double, with luscious nipples, the giant pink or chocolate penis cakes, the Sock It To Me! cakes, innuendos of plump cleavage sculpted into lemony icing. That she would have to ask, *This way or that?* about things she had never discussed either with her children or husband or her own parents—sparkles, ripples, & curves. Where the candles might go, for example, in such an instance. Who the cake should be delivered to, exactly, & what was the occasion, what words should be inscribed? It is easy to imagine her never smiling through any of these transactions, keeping a stern face, taking the money as you would touch something that had fallen into a toilet. She blamed us. Sure she did. As if we had known. The thought of these things being baked into cake had never occurred to me on this earth, even in my oddest fantasy, nor to my father; the two innocents, as we depicted ourselves during her rages. To us, the only thing to worry about in a bakery was what kind of shortening they used in the cookies or how long the cupcakes had been in the case. We had tricked her into bondage to a bakery of shame. *So quit!* we begged her. *Quit!* But her German Lutheran upbringing which said something about never running from a task once your name was on the time chart was something we could not reckon with. I think a few seasons passed. People in leopard-printed coats bought cakes for bachelor parties. Secretaries selected long cakes for wild office bashes. A mother bought a cake for her son who was turning 18. My mother glared fiercely, slamming her money down. My father & I lived in fear. Of course large numbers of people who knew nothing about the secret cakes dropped in to pick up regular sacks of cookies on their way home from the drugstore or glossy red cupcakes for a great-nephew on St. Valentine's Day—these were the people my mother lived for, the pure hearts, clean of ulterior intent. Eventually she eased back into Montessori teaching, her preferred & regular vocation. But I think she was marked by the album under the counter. It left a shadow in her spirit, a spooky truth—your most familiar people could open the door to the underworld without even knowing it & not be able to rescue you, once you toppled through. ✳

Sunday

Even though my parents had seen the French movie starring Omar Sharif in a theater and called it "very depressing," I checked it out of the library. But something was wrong with it. We pressed the English text button, the subtitles did not appear. French people were breaking piggybanks, moving in and out of neighborhood grocery stores. A teenage boy stared wistfully through the second-story window of his bedroom. We had no dialogue to connect the scenes. *Where are the words?* we kept saying. *This is kooky! Rewind it! Find the words!* But they wouldn't come up. We actually thought the movie might be too large for our screen—were the words appearing in the air below the TV set? We shrank the picture and still they didn't appear. Suddenly a sentence flashed and we sat forward in our seats—but the sentence, apparently spoken by Omar Sharif's elderly storekeeper character, was "I am not an Arab." That was it. No other text followed, even when the boy in the movie responded rapidly. I remembered how Egyptians often make a distinction between themselves and other Middle Easterners. But when the same line appeared five minutes later, spoken by another character, this time a blond woman in a tight dress, "I am not an Arab"—it seemed confusing. The same line occurred a third time, popping out of someone else's mouth—an incidental old lady character who had just walked into the grocery—"I am not an Arab"—followed, most mysteriously, by "never on a Sunday." And that was it. No other words appeared, though everyone kept talking at a rapid French pace. We wondered if the maker-of-subtitles had fallen asleep on the job, and we turned off the movie shortly thereafter. The world is too frustrating already to watch movies without any sound. And all the Arabs I know are Arabs on Monday, Tuesday, Wednesday, Thursday, etc., as well as on Sunday. Despite what the world might think, they actually like it. ❋

We Are Not Nothing

Two beads on strings
pop from a round head
on a wooden stick.
This little drum
with subtle brown skin
never forgets
his simple music.
If you roll the stick side to side
between your palms,
the beads hit the face
and the back of the face,
snap snap,
with a rhythm to it,
something old and definite,
something under the song
in a tiny Palestinian drum
shaking his humble head. ✿

Our Best Selves

Tiny folded red message:
A MILLION POUNDS OF LOVE IN THIS NOTE!
For twelve years it travels in my wallet.

In my old linen shirt, the label reads:
"All my cells are perfect spirit
doing their perfect work."
What an optimistic shirt.

But the message from my cousin
shows full-color photos
of Fallujah children sprawled
dead in a dusty street, American soldiers
leaning jauntily on tanks.
"What do we do with this sadness?"
the message pleads.
"How do we celebrate the Eid?"

I feel like my friend who once said,
"How can I ever be happy
when my brother has schizophrenia?"

O where is my mama who said,
Use words when she sent us off to school?
If someone gives you trouble,
remember your best self.
Where is my Arab father
who came to a new land
believing its language?
Where is the note of justice
tucked into history?

A billion pounds of wisdom
in this lost note.

Where is the faded tag reading
separation of church and state,
the country 'tis of US
momentarily broken in two
and the earnest son
gripping the little pencil? ❁

The Dirtiest 4-Letter Word

is "self" says the sign on a church
and I almost run off the road.

What about Kill? Hate? Rape?
Even "whip" sounds worse than "self"

or might we try "lies"? Now I remember why
Sunday School gave me a stomach *ache*. ✻

RSVP

I'm sorry.
I cannot come.
I cannot be there.
I am sure the party will be
just as good without me.
A previous engagement
with a Mottled Houdan
makes my presence impossible.
We must conduct a dance in the dust.
There's a slip of silence to be polished.
Please convey my regards.
New regard for the word *putter*,
among others.
I so much thank you
for thinking of me. ✿

Boathouse
(For E. B. White)

Isn't it only a moment ago
                   you left?

Water rippling
    giant harbor stones
thunder approaching

At your writing table we sit
on your birthday
        21 years after your departure
staring out your window
no words   all words
            you were trying to say
"you loved the world"

.   from this little shingled house
        blue door   climbing vines
            by the quiet dependable water

lobsters hand painted on table & chair

soft scratchings   pencil on pad

typewriter *tick tick*

    so beautiful *&* confusing where we are

still trying to say it ✽

The Problem of Muchness

One thing does not lead to another,
                  it leads to everything.

Days as pennies, grasses, tidal swells of speckled
     distraction,
and how could you waste time, really?
                  What did it mean to waste time?

If you stared at a soft beam of light crossing a floor,
                  was that looking wasted?

The concept of "catching up"
felt troublesome, too.
                  Catch up with what?
The yellow Post-it notes strewn across the desk?

I tried never to rush, never to think of more than
     one thing
at any given moment.
Ha.
While brushing hair I remembered unsent letters.
While feeding the cat I saw weeds wagging their
     tongues. ❋

How Do I Know
When a Poem Is Finished?

When you quietly close
the door to a room
the room is not finished.

It is resting. Temporarily.
Glad to be without you
for a while.

Now it has time to gather
its balls of gray dust,
to pitch them from corner to corner.

Now it seeps back into itself,
unruffled and proud.
Outlines grow firmer.

When you return,
you might move the stack of books,
freshen the water for the roses.

I think you could keep doing this
forever. But the blue chair looks best
with the red pillow. So you might as well

leave it that way. ✳

Excuse Me But

Did you lose a black fleece vest with green gloves in the pocket? I found it on the ground at Asilomar, California, a few years ago. Now I cannot remember if there was one green glove nestled in each zippered pocket or if the gloves were rolled up together. They seemed very new and well-chosen for the chilly evening wind by the ocean. I felt bad for whoever had lost such a durable combo, and held the items out in my hands like an offering to the young Asian man at the lobby check-in desk in the beautiful building designed by Julia Morgan. He said, "No one will claim them. Everyone from the last conference is gone. See? I have all the room keys right here. You are the only person in that building right now and no one else is expected till tomorrow. Keep those things." "But someone may claim them later," I said. "Here's my phone number back home in Texas. If anyone calls you, please call me and I'll mail them home." "They won't," he said. "No one will call. Trust me. No one. Why would they call me?" "But just in case," I pressed. "Someone will be very sad when they discover their loss. These are lovely useful things. Tape my number to your desk please. Don't let it get away."

He stared at me as if I were a zombie from zombieland interrupting his day. "I will," he said slowly. "Just in case."

Well, he never phoned and I started wearing the vest right away.

By now I have worn it in probably thirty states and five countries. We have bonded. The zippered pockets are incredibly useful on planes. Gloves still feel fairly new. I mean, global warming and all—even in Canada people barely wear gloves. But if they're yours, and you read this, I'll still send it all back to you. ❀

Bears

At breakfast we're discussing
what to do if you meet a bear
Sometimes you run
Sometimes you stand still and shout
so the bear will think you're bigger
Bears are great from a distance
ambling with cubs on a mountain trail
frolicking beside the train track
if you're safely inside the train
Grandpa bear rising up
from a distant cave
stretching his limbs
after months of hibernation
We saw one in Maine
while trying to see
a moose ❁

Pacify

Teenage boy lying asleep on a Toronto sidewalk
      over a warm air grate
at 7 in the morning
      people with briefcases & fresh shirts
      stepping neatly around
his ragged pouch & filthy pants

baby's pacifier tucked in his mouth   *Wow*
      Is it a Canadian thing?

    So strange   All day I think

how most boys that age
    wouldn't be caught dead . . .

What brought him to a chilly sidewalk
      for the night?
Where is his mother?

How many times   all mothers fail

    to be the ones our sons might need

please   someone

    protect him   on behalf of

       the family

    (for everyone's sake)

     we need to be ❀

To One Now Grown

If we could start over, I would let you get dirtier.
Place your face in the food, it's okay.

In trade for great metaphors,
the ones you used to spout every minute,
I'd extend your bedtime,
be more patient with tantrums,
never answer urgency with urgency,
try to stay serene.

In one scene you are screaming
And I stop the car.
What do we do next?
I can't remember.
It's buried in the drawer of small socks.

Give me the box of time.
Let's make it bigger.
It's all yours. ✳

Watch Your Language

Pleasant words are a honeycomb,
sweet to the soul
and healing to the bones.

   –Proverbs 16:24

A militant is not a man
who orders stealth bombers
to devastate a neighborhood.
He has a lot of money
so he is not a militant.
A militant is a man
whose 14-year-old son
was killed last week.
He is now out of his mind.
He could do something dangerous
and he has no money at all.
Watch him. ✽

Cat Plate

That's what we used to do in our house,
says Lydia, when we were mad at our dad—
we served him on the cat plate.
He didn't know, since he never fed the cat.
It made us laugh secretly in the kitchen—
the plate had a crack so maybe
some cat saliva had stuck in there.
It gave us a little buzz.

Once when he was being really mean,
he grabbed what he thought was tuna in
   a glass container
but it was cat food. Our mother, washing dishes,
froze with her mouth wide open when she realized—
I shook my head, finger on my lips.
From the living room he said, *This tuna*
has taken on a new taste.
No one told him.

We just did our homework silently
at the kitchen table
and grinned when we caught each other's eye.
There were all kinds of ways
we felt better about our lives back then
and sometimes they surprised us. ❄

Click

The birthday party day unexpectedly holds
a funeral, too, Dutch chocolate torte layered
with *His Eye Is on the Sparrow*.
Buddhist wedding ceremony, same day
H and P decide to split.
Comfort's General Store burns down
right before our neighbor's house is robbed.
One million acres of the Texas Panhandle
flaming, ten thousand animals
scorched. Three people told me
poetry saved their lives, on the same day
they told me this. ❋

Hibernate

*

My father's friend Farouk
has a dream:
God resigned.
And all the people took better care of one another
and got together then
because, well, they had to.
Things grew really smooth.
There was no one to blame or impress.

*

Professor Brother Miguel Angel
is healing "mexican style"
every day of the week for free.
He is healing "different from others."
He will "run away bad neighbors"
if you ask him to. Note: he stuck his
promotional poster on your neighbor's house
as well as your own.
He will "bring back boyfriends"
and "give names of persons."
Call for appointment
night or day. Good luck for Bingo,

too. Bingo is capitalized,
mexican is not. I want
brown magic this year.
Brown dusty desert magic.
I want peace even if it involves
a lot of weeping and apology.
Can you help me? Keep
your Bingo joy, I need real
people lighting sage sticks,
being honest. Say *disaster*.
Thank you.

*

Spring feels different this year.
It's a bandage.
Mountain laurel . . . jasmine . . .
The wound keeps oozing, though.

*

I keep thinking how the man who said
100 Arabs don't equal 1 American

was wearing a white shirt
and had seemed perfectly normal
up till then.

*

Favorite questions from the FBI:

*In all your travels, have you ever met
anyone who used an assumed name?*

Uh, it *is* possible Abdul Faisal Shamsuzzaman
was really Jack Smith, but how would I know?

*In all your travels, did you ever meet anyone
who wanted to overthrow their country?*

Hmmmm, would they have announced it?

Yes.   Me.   Now.

*

The turtles who live with us emerge from hibernation
on the first day of Official Spring.

How do they know?
And where were they for the whole iffy winter?
In which bed of leaves did they bury
themselves?

On the first Official Day,
they climbed heavily back into their old red tub
lifting reptilian heads above water,
blinking slowly . . .
we were so ready to feed them.

*

It's awkward to be with people sometimes,
making shapes in the air
that feel like sense—
I'd rather talk to J. Frank Dobie
who died years ago.

Lucille remembers him sitting
in a white linen suit
on her grandfather's South Texas porch,
stories spinning like spiders
along the wooden beams . . .

*

Homeland Security wanted to know
what those mysterious silver objects were,
entering my cousin's home—
trays of *tabouleh*
covered with aluminum foil.

*

Logic hibernates.
Truth, too.
It has been known to stay gone
for years. ❃

My President Went

quail hunting
to celebrate the advent
of a new year.
He didn't kill many birds
only five,
but called it "lots of fun."
Each bird had lungs
and fancy feathers
and elegant strong feet.

People who study quail
describe their
"small family groups,"
how some species prefer
to crouch and hide in tall grass
while others
"fly in the face of danger."

There are many things
my president might have done
after months of killing and sorrow
but he chose to take a gun
into the fields.

Note: I wrote this poem before my vice-president shot his friend in the face
while quail hunting in south Texas. The above poem also happened in Texas.
Sometimes when young writers ask what triggers poems, I could just hold
up a daily newspaper, which still costs fifty cents except on Sundays in many
cities. ❁

Texas Swing Low

JESUS IS THE KING OF CUERO
trumpets a billboard on Highway 87 South.
I wonder, is it enough,
would He be glad to hear this?
And what about Smiley and Pandora,
is He just a prince there, or perhaps
a backup band? And Stockdale's signs
seem devoted to the Internet.
In brisk December, Victoria and Goliad
pray barbeque will come around again
on the Sunday grill.

New holiday trend in coastal bend:
bare wooden crosses in bare front yards.
But isn't that Easter?
Jesus doesn't get a lot of say.
Jesus is the king of the toy box.
Jesus misses the old days.

A lone ostrich stands
in a windswept overgrown brown field
behind the faded EXOTICS sign
tacked to her fence.
INFO ON HUNTING it says.
Then a telephone number she can't dial
from this life or the next. ✿

From an Island

One quick blip of Internet
After days of disconnection
Streak of startling lines
Train blown up in India
Someone famous dies
Guerilla actions
Military movements
Bridges bombed
Buckets and bags of sadness
Don't want
Don't want to know
any of it
Want any?
No ✿

The White Cat

I never heard his name. Does he have a name?

Right before I rose to give a public lecture in Cairo, in a room far too fancy for a simple person like myself—ornate carvings in the ceiling, Oriental rugs, fine intricate windows—a white cat walked confidently down the center aisle of the hall and stepped onto the platform at the front, where I was being introduced. He looked at me, with an "Ah, there you are!" look and sat right beside me while I gave my talk. I had looked up the word "lecture" in the dictionary beforehand and discovered the source of the quiver in my stomach—"lecture" means something stern someone gives you, a life lesson sort of thing. Also, a formal reproof, a reprimand.
No thanks.
I didn't have that. I had scrambled bits and pieces, poems, quotes, a weird outfit, bits of paper written on by 8-year-olds, and a vagrant white cat. Somehow the cat—most pure discourse offered that afternoon—never entered the comments I made to the audience, which in retrospect seems strange. It is so easy to make a joke out of something right next to you. But there was a sanctity about him. There was also the chance I was

the only one seeing him. He seemed ghostly and I felt quite disembodied and no one else *was looking at him.* He just sat there, then left at the end of the talk, stepping neatly out of the room. I did not see him for the next week. Dodging all over Cairo in wild taxicabs and the underground Metro, riding a *fellucca* sailboat on the Nile at sundown, stomping here and there, I saw many other cats (Cairo is famous for cats) but not that one. Till I was preparing to leave the school campus where I had worked—over by one of the security stations (where only days before I had a slight fracas with a security agent who wanted to hold on to my passport, which I did not like—*What if he took off with it? What if I needed identification while on campus?*), the same white cat rose out of some low bushes, sleepily, and stepped over the cobblestones daintily to press against my legs.

In two simple acts of movement, he welcomed me to campus and told me farewell. It is difficult to predict what our finest moments will be, but we know when they happen. ✳

Ducks in Couples

Four pairs of ducks
Swimming in strong circles
In the lake
Heads down
Kicking hard

Four perfect clots of spinning duck
In perfect harmonic movement
Trying to lift the bits of tasty debris
From the bottom of the lake

I didn't know this at first
Thought a mating ritual might be underway
But discovered later what they were doing
On that day when human beings in the world
Continued to kill one another
Because their imaginations
Were broken sticks
Without any feathers ❋

Campaigning Door to Door

Maybe we will not

      vote

no candidate is worth   US

      we are

           patriotic Americans

guarding our precious American   gloom

      pinned to our screens

         and incomplete yard projects

        Who?   BEAT IT!

When is

early voting?   No   I did not

think about it   yet   I have a lot

on my mind

You can't get   me

to do

anything

Parents of Murdered Palestinian Boy Donate His Organs to Israelis

Ahmed Ismail Khatib, you died,
but you have so many bodies now.
You became a much bigger boy.
You became a girl too—
your kidneys, your liver, your heart.
So many people needed what you had.

In a terrible moment,
your parents pressed against
spinning cycles of revenge
to do something better.
They stretched.
What can that say to the rest of us?

In the photograph your hand
is raised to your chin—position of thought.
This was not your intention.
But people you will never meet are cheering.

Please keep telling us something true.

Because of your kidneys, your liver, your heart—
we must—simply *must*—be bigger too. ❀

Before I Read *The Kite Runner*

I held it on my lap on the plane in Cairo while other passengers were boarding. It seemed like a good book to read, finally, on such a long flight. I'd had it since it came out, but now the time felt right. Two men from Yemen across the aisle, who had been snoozing when the Egypt passengers first boarded, pointed and said, "Good book! Good book!" Some women from Germany patted my head and said, "We loved that book." An American man with his wife leaned over and said, "It opened our eyes." What a surprise! Everyone on the plane seemed to have read it before me. And they were all my friends simply because I was holding it!

Maybe we should just wander around other countries carrying books. ✽

The First Time I Was Old

The sky crackled
with scary lightning.
Our fuel tank
had to be drained and refilled
before the plane could fly.
I said "Hi" to the 20-ish guy
taking the next seat.
He had bumped a woman
across the aisle
saying, "Sorry! My elbow,"
so I know he spoke English.
He took one long look at me
and decidedly
didn't answer. ❀

Useless

Threat alert at airport is

ORANGE

Okay

    I'll put on my orange personality

    orange gaze

    for faces all around me

for paper bags stashed next to
    not in

    the rubbish bin ✽

Jonathan's Kiwi Cake

From the side it's a sculpture
arcs of kiwi
small green doors
almond glaze streaking across top
He's a genius
but don't tell him that
They say he doesn't like to be noticed
Could that be true?

I love his photographs, too
layerings of people
rich icings of city crowds
"shot from the hip" he says
"rather literally"
He doesn't say much more

The cakes were lined up on the dessert table
when we came to lunch
Jonathan had disappeared
gone back to the small cottage he lives in
so he wouldn't have to say
you're welcome   you're welcome   you're welcome ✿

Consolation

This morning the newspaper
was too terrible to deliver
so the newsboy just pitched out
a little sheaf
of Kleenex. ❀

For Rudolf Staffel

Your trough was crammed with chips & bits,
pieces of fired porcelain, broken things.
"They're my teachers," you said kindly,
    tipping your hat.

On any street, in any crowded room,
you saw beyond the visible shapes.
"Where are you from?" It was always earth

we are all from, but forget—
you held it, listened to its breath,
found its fluent curve.

And what you became was a new way of being.
What you touched, the openhearted vessels
brilliant, bold, and true.

You weren't afraid to experiment,
swerve. Giving freely, translating radiance,
all you knew. Conveying it

so anyone in your presence loved their own lives
and anything they had seen or might be, more.
You were the window the light came through. ❊

Hot Stone Massage

Because my body has been
rubbed with hot black stones
I will now be able to grow older
with dignity.

It was easy to sense
the soil and dust
we all become
somewhere in the hot heart
of stone memory
and it wasn't scary at all.

It was more home than home.

There were no chores. ❀

Regular Days

Look at those mansions,
don't you wish one was yours?
Actually, I like little houses,
less to clean. I wanted to live under the roots
of a tree, like the squirrel family in a picture book,
when I was small.
I'm still the kid dreaming of the lives she'll never have
but guess what?
Maybe she doesn't want them.
Some houses wear their Christmas lights
till February 6. I always feel like celebrating
when everything is over. I belong to
the secret clot of renegades
that prefers regular days. Trash days
really excite me. ✳

Last Day of School

The long yellow pencils with promising pointed tips, shrunken to nubs. Trash cans overflow. We've turned in the thick books, though we know there was a lot we skimmed over quickly. Those final chapters, the modern days. We're feeling fond of the grumpy teacher, the smoky chalk groove along the blackboard's rim. Running our fingers along everything we can—nicks in the wooden tops of our desks, snappy rings of a crowded notebook, as we stuff the final papers in, the cool edge of the metal chair. Our many minor mistakes erased the high hopes of far-gone September. We were going to be perfect. We were going to make all *A*s. Today someone who didn't speak to us all year—Freddy? Steve?—speaks suddenly, comfortably, and it is so clear—we could have been friends. We were here all along. The black and white marquee at the edge of the schoolyard says LAST DAY OF SCHOOL JUNE 2. We pin things to that date. A deeper breath, gulp of finer air, extended evenings in the back lot playing Lost in the Forest, or Gone from Here. I'm fond of the game called

Families Getting Along. Soft light, peach cobbler, fireflies, a colander of fresh-picked cherries. Our school paintings return to us slightly battered. We smooth their corners. The classroom walls grow emptier by the hour. Someone agrees to take the turtle home.

There are moments we stand back from our classmates and teacher and familiar territory as if trying to contain the details of the scene precisely, in case we need to find our ways here again. Central School, you will remain central in my compass, your red-brick certitude, your polished ancient halls. I have marched and circled and bent my head inside you. I have wandered and lost my way. I have been proud, been locked in, been shy, been wounded by a vagrant strip of metal in a doorway, and stitched back together, been punished. In second grade I spoke into the recently installed intercom, to say my first published poem to the whole school at once, and this phenomenon was more exciting than seeing the poem in the magazine. If my lips touched the silver microphone I might be electrocuted. I was never invited to speak into it again though there were many other things I might have said. I pray to Central School as much as I pray to any God or gods.

I believe in the tall windows, the rounded porcelain drinking trough. I love eating on a tray. When my parents fight, when my mother locks herself in her bedroom for hours, sobbing, and I press my ear to the door to make sure she is still alive, when my father disappears into the city, I know the school building five blocks from our house has not changed a bit. It would still comfort me if I stepped into it.

It is true I have little interest in the future. When teachers speak of ambition, college, goals, careers, success, my eyes are trailing dust motes in a beam of sun. I want everyone to leave the room so I can go through the trash. Maybe there is something in there I could use right now.

Kindergarten through sixth grade, the school knows us. The school is our stable and we are little horses dashing up the hill to beat the bell every morning. My father is the only Arab father, but he runs for PTA president and is elected. The French Canadian and Italian parents vote for him. He runs for school board later and loses. "I think that was pushing it," says my mother. What does "pushing it" mean? Thinking about the future is pushing it. I would hold us here even when Here hurts, but nothing gives me that power. Only in words on a page can it still be yesterday. Still Walt Whitman, still Abraham Lincoln, Susan B. Anthony, only in words. There were more chapters in that book, I'm sure of it. More tribes and countries we had not discussed.

What I cannot dream then is how I will come back to Central School on the day after the Last Day, 40 years later. The custodian pausing in the same front doorway with his wide broom, a dreamy relaxed look on his face. He says, Go right in, it's still there. Look around. Don't tell anyone I haven't emptied the trash cans yet.

I take my time. It's summer, so that's all there is. Because Central School is a historic monument to more people than me, nothing really has changed. Same drinking trough. Same banister and wide stairs. I paw through the trash can in my second grade classroom and claim *My Personal Dictionary* by Eric—the "L" page lists "Light, Love, Laugh, Lift, Lose, Little, Loose, Labor." Okay Eric, I say out Loud. A+, man. Everything you'll need for the Life, man, right there on one page. I stick his dictionary in my waistband under my T-shirt, feeling like a pirate, press my forehead against the white bathroom wall tile, down low, where I would have reached in third grade. I did not mean to break John's nose or drive Miss Dreon crazy. I should never *ever* have told Karen to pull down her underpants on the playground. In the gymnasium, the same stage I stood on, could it be, the same burgundy draperies? I shoot a few free throws and make them. I never made them back then. A ring of ghostly girls dances a Gypsy dance. Didn't we wear our grandmothers' scarves? And didn't we pledge, pledge, pledge, palms on our chests, every day we lived, pledge to the one nation, the freedom we believed in, didn't we? Fat lot of good.

Forty years later I want to be true to that oddball in a golden gunny-sack dress with purple sleeves. What history taught us, we promised to learn. We would be braver, wiser, than ones who came before. We pledged, and felt proud in the pledging. There would be no more war because the world had seen war, it was terrible and now we knew better things. We would always be rich in our knowing, even if our velvet sacks of quarters gave out, and our mothers' sorrow turned to anger, and our principal went to jail. There were extra red bricks stacked in the corners of our yard, same color as the school. There could still be a project. We would do better this time.

Slow time rapidly passing, watch it, the time we can't believe till a few years after my return to Central School, we're sitting in another auditorium clapping for our own boy crossing a stage on his high school graduation day. He could not find the red tassel for his flat hat, so he is wearing my old black one, the only graduate with a black one. Tomorrow I will find the red tassel in the trash, still in the plastic, at home. Care in the details, I always told him. It didn't take. I was a better student than mother, maybe. And now it is too late for new habits. And the headlines count the boys, the men, the women, fallen every day for stupid reasons, cycles of falling, the headlines count and they do not count, and I despise them. Pledging to nothing but what can't be said, to Lost Labor and the Light we smother, for what? We're pushing it.

A thousand miles from the first city, and the parents still fighting in the foyer of my boy's graduation hall, who could believe it? The parents still fighting, like history I guess, old repetitions unresolved, and the books still closing and history's oiled engine clicking and spinning. All over the city of my grown-up years, marquees announcing farewell at every front gate and playground, wishing us well, wishing us a good summer even though you have to look really hard for a firefly now. I blow kisses to every one of them, tears in my eyes and throat and nose, I was a fool, and I will always be a fool, and there will never, never, be a last day of school. ✿

Young Drummer Leaving Alamo Music Company

Slapping wooden sticks against your hand
with the pride that says, "These are mine,
I know how to use them," walking beside your father
and brother in the stark July heat one early evening,
and I felt the lost sticks inside my own heart rat-a-tat
    a little beat
back over to you though of course you didn't hear it
thinking about fathers and mothers who are nice
    enough
to let their kids take drum lessons even when it is
    the last instrument
they would like to hear inside their house and I heard
    your daddy say,
"You gotta practice, son, I really mean practice"
and I wondered, was that your first lesson? Are you
    still full of the hope
of becoming a great drummer or was that
    your 20th lesson
and the teacher just said, "Where's that riff I told you
    to learn?"
You looked proud. Drummers are always proud.
    I was so proud

even though I only had a practice pad and got kicked
   out of marching band
for some forgotten reason (may you have a better
   career),
but hear me now. Even if you give it all up, as I did,
even if you don't hold sticks for twenty years,
on some steamy night in Texas long down the road
when you've lost two friends in a week and didn't say
   good-bye
to either of them, when you're staring straight ahead
at things getting worse in the world, wishing
   everybody could hear
their own distant drummer playing *anything better*,
you realize, you are still hitting odd rhythmic patterns
on the skin of this world and in all the strange,
   familiar ways,
it is still hitting you. ❁

The Room in Which We Are Every Age at Once

As if there were
a home in the air around us from birth,
spaciousness bidding us enter,
we live inside the long story of time.
And it was language giving us bearing,
letting in light.
When I was 3, sky rimming pink
above rooftops,
Grandpa planted a redbud tree
that would bloom for years beyond us.
Each year it would say spring first.

Vocabulary falling into place,
we were always old and young
feeling familiar lines resound,
my favorite Margaret Wise Brown,
who died right before I was born,
and precious solitary Emily D.,
the words of all time waiting,
latched together like small huts,
stories of wise animals
and human beings
rising up inside us
to shelter our days. ✼

Gate A-4

Wandering around the Albuquerque Airport Terminal, after learning my flight had been delayed four hours, I heard an announcement: "If anyone in the vicinity of Gate A-4 understands any Arabic, please come to the gate immediately."

Well—one pauses these days. Gate A-4 was my own gate. I went there.

An older woman in full traditional Palestinian embroidered dress, just like my grandma wore, was crumpled to the floor, wailing loudly. "Help," said the flight service person. "Talk to her. What is her problem? We told her the flight was going to be late and she did this."

I stooped to put my arm around the woman and spoke to her haltingly. "Shu-dow-a, Shu-bid-uck Habibti? Stani schway, Min fadlick, Shu-bit-se-wee?" The minute she heard any words she knew, however poorly used, she stopped crying. She thought the flight had been cancelled entirely. She needed to be in El Paso for major medical treatment the next day. I said, "No, we're fine, you'll get there, just later, who is picking you up? Let's call him."

We called her son and I spoke with him in English. I told him I would stay with his mother till we got on the plane and would ride next to her—Southwest. She talked to him. Then we called her other sons just for the fun of it. Then we called my dad and he and she spoke for a while in Arabic and found out of course they had ten shared friends. Then I thought just for the heck of it why not call some Palestinian poets I know and let them chat with her? This all took up about two hours.

She was laughing a lot by then. Telling about her life, patting my knee, answering questions. She had pulled a sack of homemade *mamool* cookies—little powdered sugar crumbly mounds stuffed with dates and nuts—out of her bag—and was offering them to all the women at the gate. To my amazement, not a single woman declined one. It was like a sacrament. The traveler from Argentina, the mom from California, the lovely woman from Laredo—we were all covered with the same powdered sugar. And smiling. There is no better cookie.

✳✳

And then the airline broke out free beverages from huge coolers and two little girls from our flight ran around serving us all apple juice and they were covered with powdered sugar, too. And I noticed my new best friend—by now we were holding hands—had a potted plant poking out of her bag, some medicinal thing, with green furry leaves. Such an old country traveling tradition. Always carry a plant. Always stay rooted to somewhere.

And I looked around that gate of late and weary ones and thought, This is the world I want to live in. The shared world. Not a single person in that gate—once the crying of confusion stopped—seemed apprehensive about any other person. They took the cookies. I wanted to hug all those other women, too.

This can still happen anywhere. Not everything is lost. ✿